TIME
TO:
GO
WILD

MW00815512

STORY DESCRIPTION:
The King of Snizz is building a royal sanctuary for rare animals in honor of the Crown Prince's upcoming wedding. When the bride arrives for the big event, the Prince, who is also the kingdom's zoologist, goes undercover in disguise to see if this one-of-a-kind creature will adapt to her new surroundings.

ISBN-13:978-1492163176
ISBN-10:1492163171

ZOOPOSSIBLE!
Royal Kingdom

WRITTEN & ILLUSTRATED BY
LOLA LOMBARD
AND YOU!

To the great storytellers in my family,
Ron Wohl, Marc Spiegel,
Louis Chevelier, Anabelle Lombard.

Thank you to my friends and family
who supported the efforts of
publishing this story.

HI!

It's me, Lola, the author-illustrator of this book!

Welcome to ZOOPOSSIBLE, where the wild ideas roam free!

I made this book just for you, so you can help this adventure come alive! You can insert your own ideas, drawings, and explanations inside this book on the pages where we ask you to doodle. If you want to change your ideas, feel OK to tape in pages of your own, right on top or into the back. All your ideas will be unique and amazing because inside you is a creative genius! There is one in each of us. So grab a pencil or pen and follow me to the next page. Something's happening...

THE KING OF SNIZZ sat in his castle

listening to his Jester suggest how to tell his son the big news.

"Er... great news, Son. You've been invited to a wedding. As the groom!"

"Hmm. No. Too sneaky," said the King.

The Jester dashed out and then returned wearing tropical flowers and a grass skirt. He tried again. "Hey, nice weather we are having, eh? Anyone for a surprise wedding?"

The king shook his head. "Uh, well, maybe this might be better told to him in a letter." he said. He grabbed some parchment and in his kingly script he scribbled,

Dear Son — You've been arranged in marriage to the Princess of Belkenbop, from over the mountaintop. You'll be married by the end of the week.

"No, no, no," thought the King. "This is my one and only son. A letter is too cowardly. I'm the King of Snizz. I'll just have to break the news quite bluntly. I'll call him forth, put on the razzamatazz, and just blurt it out!"

THE KING SUMMONED HIS COURAGE, AS THE ROYAL TRUMPETS OF SNIZZ CALLED FORTH THE PRINCE.

"DO, DA, DOO!" blared the trumpets, and the Prince appeared, as usual in his Royal Snizz Zoologist camouflage vest and cap, with notebook, pen, magnifying glass, binoculars, jar, net, and tweezers.

"Hey, Dad!" said the Prince. "Just look at this new species of Snoozfly I've spotted today! That makes our hundred and fifty - fourth species of rare creatures! It's fascinating! I found it resting on the forest floor between snoozes! But it can't fly now. I think it might have hurt its wing. I am going to watch it carefully to learn more about it and then release it safely back into the forest when it's ready."

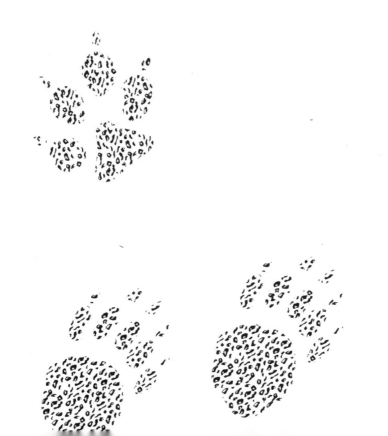

Mom

Chance

DOODLE /DESCRIBE THE RARE SNOOZFLY

The King glanced at the Snoozfly and smiled. He looked into the eyes of his son with great fatherly love as he thought of the best way to spill the beans. "I am so proud of your curiosity and your kindness, my son. And I know that you are ready for ..."

"LUNCH!" said the Prince. "I'm starving! Let's go!"

"In a minute, my son. But I was going to say, I know you are ready for...marriage!" The King flashed a smile and put on his *razzamatazz.* "I have arranged your marriage ceremony for this Friday. It shall be a day the kingdom will always remember!" And then the King danced about wildly.

"Marriage?" The Prince just stood there, stunned!

"Sure," said the King. I feel that you are ready to care for people now, not just the animals of Snizz! And in honor of your wedding, we'll build an animal sanctuary for our rarest of rare animals and hold the wedding ceremony in front of its gates! Snizz shall forever be a place where the people and the animals can live in beautiful harmony. WE'LL CALL IT ZOOPOSSIBLE!"

7

"WOW! ZOOPOSSIBLE! Maybe you are right. Maybe I am ready," said the Prince, sounding curious about the newest species that would be entering the kingdom. "So who is this lovely and beautiful creature you've picked to be my bride?"

The King relaxed a bit when the Prince seemed to take the news so well (but then, of course, the Prince hadn't met her yet). The King hoped that the Prince would have patience with his new bride. She was a quite unusual choice for the Prince, but she was the only choice for miles around. So she would have to do.

"It's the Princess Belkenbop from over the mountaintop. I don't think you've ever been there before," said the King. " And this will be her first time to the Kingdom of Snizz."

"I cannot wait to meet her!" said the Prince. "I know she'll be so sweet and kind and love me and my animals! We'll all live together..."

"...in a harmonica!" said the Jester, excitedly juggling musical instruments.

"No, Jester, in harmony, peaceful togetherness. I know it will be a perfect match," said the Prince.

"Great," said the King. "I'm glad you feel that way. For tomorrow she will be here!"

The next day, the Prince and the Jester were
in the castle garden looking for creatures
when they heard strange, high - pitched
noises and saw something sparkly on the
other side of the bushes! "Let's sneak up and
observe it," whispered the Prince to the Jester.
The Prince whipped out his binoculars.

"Yeah, yeah, my wedding day is nearly here!" She squealed into her cell phone. "There will be a great feast, extravagant royal clothes, and expensive presents, especially jewels! And all this land and all the things in this land will be mine! Oh goody! Isn't this great?"

She continued without even catching her breath, "I can't wait to go shopping for the wedding! In honor of my wedding, great new things will be built for the whole kingdom to enjoy!" she said into the cell phone, "Ohhhhh, now that could only mean one thing! A great big shopping mall!" she squealed with delight,

"I'm going to love it here!"

Back behind the bush, the Jester whispered to the Prince, "It's an animal, all right! It's a 'Bridezilla!' She won't be happy living here in Snizz!"

"And I don't think I'll be happy living forever with her!" the Prince whispered back. "I think we'll need to observe her in her new habitat, Jester. Go out there and talk to her, but don't tell her I am watching!" whispered the Prince.

So the Jester jumped out from the hiding spot and did a CARTWHEEL in front of the Princess.

"You must be the Bride from Belkenbop! I am Jester," he bowed, "here to make you smile and laugh! I have a riddle just for you!"

"I love riddles," she said, as she hung up the cell phone without even saying goodbye.

"What's big and furry and filled with people?" joked the Jester.

"A fur shop in a shopping mall?" asked the Princess, clapping her hands with glee!

"No, Princess, it's ZOOPOSSIBLE! — a new animal sanctuary being built in honor of your wedding!" said the Jester. "And that makes you a royal Zookeeper!"

"No shopping mall? Me a Zookeeper? I'm freaking out!" cried the Princess.

"Yup, I'll be sneaking out," said the Jester.

"Where do you think you're going?" asked the Princess.

"I heard you say sneak out," the Jester replied.

"Freak out!" the Princess cried.

"OK!" said the Jester, and he proceeded to throw his arms all about.

"Wahhh! What am I going to do?" she asked herself. She looked at the Jester. "Be gone!" she commanded.

But Jester made fun again, panting like a dog with his tongue and paws out begging.

"UGGHH! I DID NOT SAY BEG ON, I SAID BE GONE!

Oh, forget it!" and the Princess ran off back to the castle teetering on her sparkly high heels, with the Jester barking close behind her.

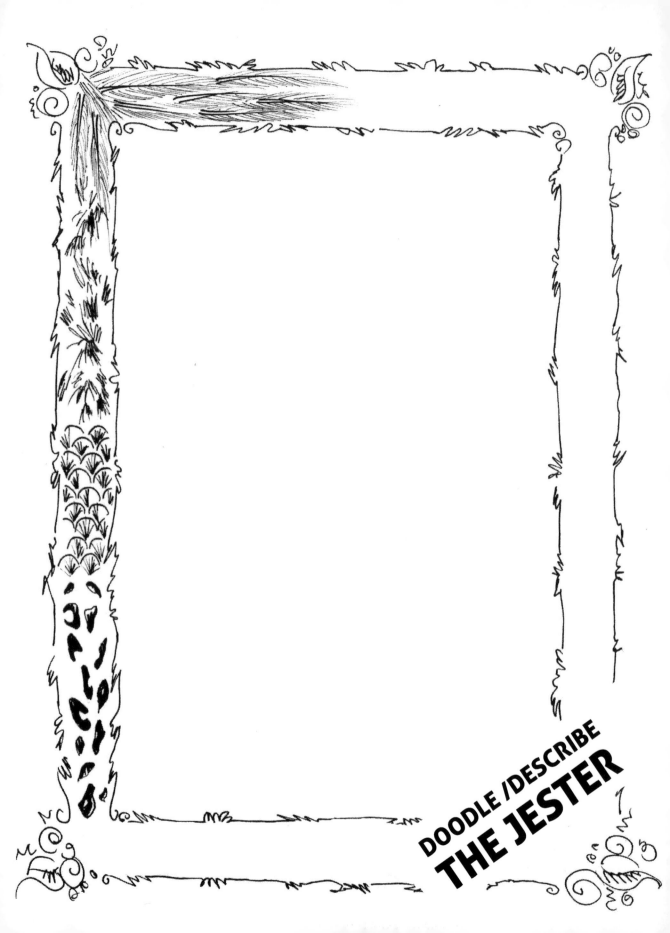

DOODLE /DESCRIBE
THE JESTER

The Jester chased the Princess all the way to her new room at the castle. Then standing back up on his feet he said, "I hope you will like it here in Snizz!" And then he left her to unpack. The Princess placed her pink sparkly things around her room to make it feel more like home.

"Ewww gross, a Zookeeper?

Zookeepers get dirty! A Princess does not get dirty! We have nice, clean things. And we get anything we want. I want to stop this zoo from being built. How can I do that? Let's see," she thought to herself. "They can't have a zoo without any animals! I'll have to find ways to get rid of those pooping pests before the wedding. Then I can have my giant shopping mall and everything else my heart desires!"

Luckily, the Jester was listening right outside the door and heard every whiney word. He cartwheeled as fast as he could to the Prince's side of the castle, where the Prince was in his room, talking to himself.

"I can't marry someone who wants to turn our animal sanctuary into a shopping mall! What will I do? How can I stop the wedding? Let's see, they can't have a wedding without a groom! That's it," he said. "I'll run away!"

The Jester cartwheeled into the room and laughed. "That's a terrible idea! Then she'd be here and you'd be gone!" He leapt to his feet, and with one finger in the air he said, "What if this animal could adapt to her new environment? Maybe she'd be happy here, your highness."

"You're right!" said the Prince. "Maybe she can adapt. I know just what we'll do! I'll pretend to go missing." While I am missing, I can be in disguise and learn more about her. And you can help me with everything!

Quick, to the royal costume vault!"

Meanwhile, all that devious scheming up in her room was making the Princess hungry. Being a resourceful Princess, she used her hunger in her plan.

"Can I get some lunch in here?" she screamed.
The Prince was a step ahead of her, already disguised as the Royal Chef.

"How can I help you, Princess?" asked the Prince.
The Princess thought about the rarest of animals in the kingdom. "I would like a rare snarklecat sandwich!"

"You are aware that there is only one snarkelcat left in the whole kingdom? "

"Exactly," said the Princess, "and it looks so juicy!"

"Perhaps I can interest you in something a little more popular? Peanut butter and jelly, maybe?"

The Princess grew furious! She was used to getting her way. "I WANT A SNARKLECAT SANDWICH! The last of the snarklecats will make this sandwich extra delicious and one of a kind, like me!"

"Yes, your Princesslyness, I will make you a sandwich at once." When the Princess was not looking, he winked at the Jester standing in the hall, and he said "I'll go catch it for you now."

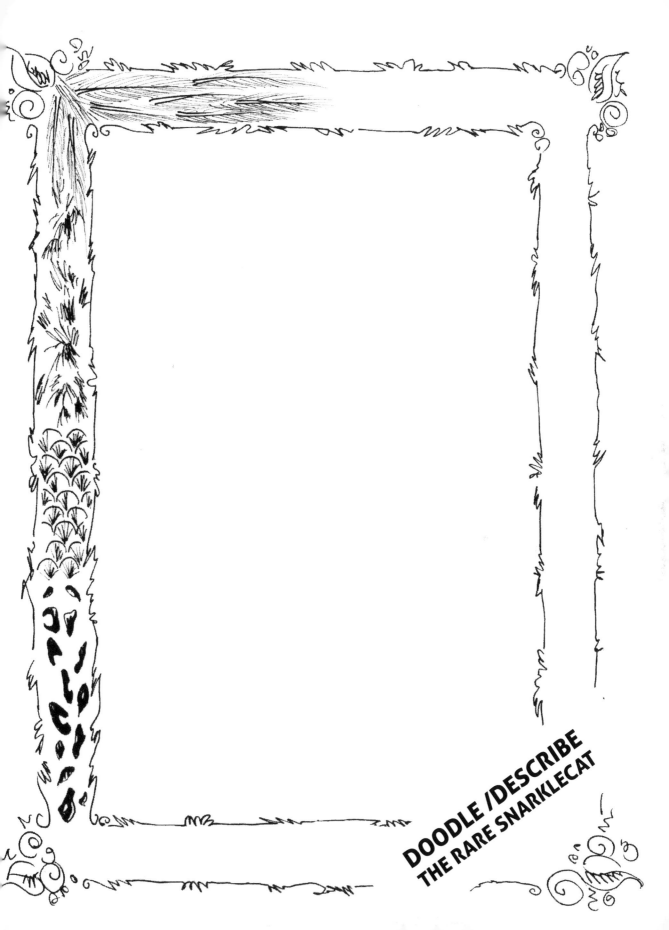

DOODLE /DESCRIBE THE RARE SNARKLECAT

"Finally!" she screamed as the Chef left the room. "That will be one less animal for their silly zoo!"

"So she wants a snarklecat sandwich, hmmmm" thought the Prince. " I simply won't cook one of our rare animals," he said to the Jester. "I'll serve her something else and make it taste like snarkelcat."

Just then the King passed in the hall on his way to greet the Princess. He saw the Chef and the Jester outside the Princess's room. "Say, have you seen my son? I can't find him anywhere. If you see him, please tell him to get ready for his wedding. The Princess is here!"

The next day, the Jester was juggling for the Princess when her stomach started to make gurgling sounds. It reminded the Princess she could ask for another rare animal meal! "Wow, that sandwich I had yesterday was so delicious!" she said. "We don't have animals like that in my kingdom. They are all gone. Jester, I demand that I be served a new animal for every meal! Go tell the Chef to get me very meaty meals!"

"SPEEDY EELS! The eels in Snizz are very rare. We have 'eels on wheels,' Princess. They are quite speedy that way!" said the Jester.

"What????" said the Princess. "Not speedy eels. Meaty meals, you ridiculous goofball!" she yelled. "Meals! Meals! Tell the Chef to keep those meals coming!" and she pushed the Jester out the door to fetch the Chef. When the Princess was all alone, she began scheming once again. "Now, how else can I get rid of some of those animals? I know, DREAM HOMES!" She smiled. "I already will live in a castle, but if they won't be building a shopping mall, I will have them build homes for me all over this kingdom! I'll have a beach house, a skyscraper with a tower, a cliff home, a mountain home, and more! I'll have one that looks like shoes, and one in the shape of a crown, and one in the shape of a rare animal sandwich!! Why not!"

"Jester!!!!" she cried out,

"Bring in the Royal Architect!"

The Jester was back in a flash, with the Prince in disguise once more. "Hello, Princess. I am the Royal Architect. I understand you wish to build a dwelling!"

"Yes, I do," she said. "Many!"

"But you already will be living in the most beautiful castle in all the land," he said. "The Palace of Snizz has everything that anyone would ever need already."

"It's not enough for me," she said. "I want to see the mountains, the beaches, the stars, and the city all from my room. So you'll have to build me many, many homes!"

"But this will uproot all the rare animals in our kingdom by digging up their habitats," said the Royal Architect.

"Well, sometimes these things are needed. I am the only Princess in Snizz. I have needs. I need these homes. Now please, go and be as creative as you can. And make it QUICK!" she replied, extra loudly.

"You bet, Princess. I promise it will be quite creative, and you'll soon see the mountains, the beaches, the stars, and the city from your room." And off he went with a wink and a funny smile.

"Hmmm, that was strange," said the Princess.

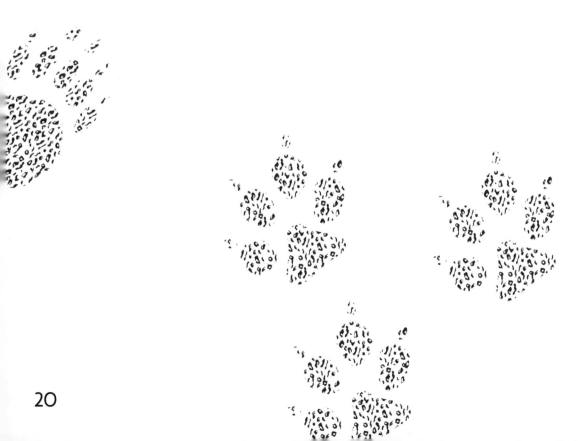

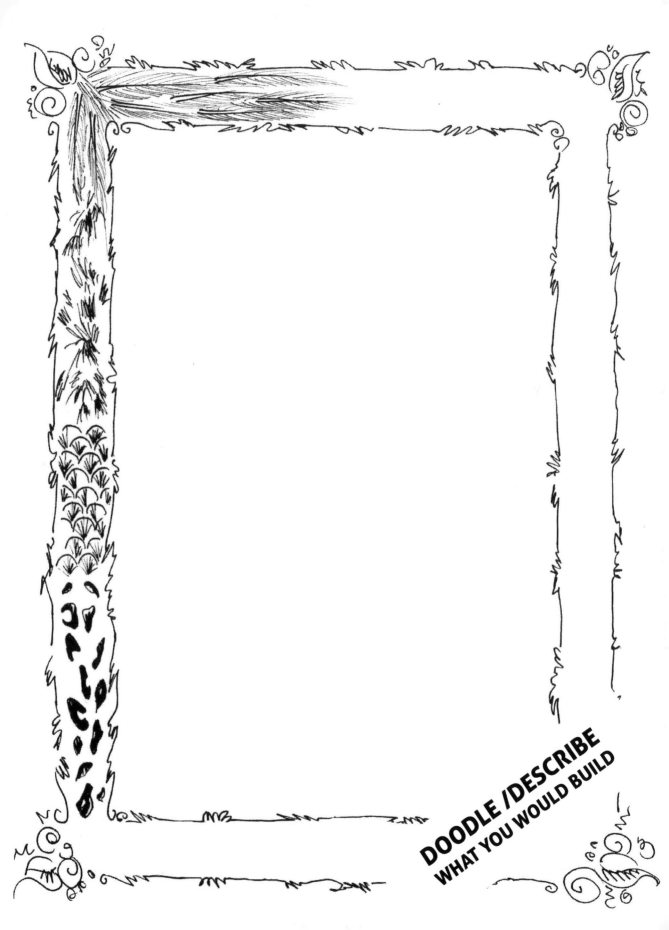

DOODLE /DESCRIBE
WHAT YOU WOULD BUILD

"This is going well! I can continue with my plan," remarked the Princess. "Jester, "Bring in the Royal Designer!"

"You called, Madame," said the Prince, disguised as the Royal Designer in a groovy hat, dark glasses, and a long scarf.

"Yes. I want some new royal clothes made for my wedding day! Something wonderful made from, um, you know, um, rare royal animals!"

"Princess, I am sure you would not want to wear rare creatures of Snizz. Who would live in our new Royal Sanctuary?" he asked.

The Princess turned red and said, "These animals may be one of a kind. But so am I. I am a royal Princess and I need to wear something that no one else in the whole kingdom would have. It has to be very special! And you must make it for me."

"Yes, your highness, it's true, you are one of a kind, all right!"

"And don't forget my jewels, even if you have to dig holes all over the kingdom to mine them!"

"I'll get right to work immediately to make you something that will feature your beauty!"

"Yes!" she said.

"And your grace."

"Yes," she cooed.

"Your charm."

"Yes," she blushed.

"I'll make something," he giggled, "that will be one of a kind!"

"Hmmm... I am getting to like this place!" said the Princess.

The Prince left the Princess's room with a huge smile. "This is working out great!" he said to Jester. "Every day we go out and catch an animal and take it to the castle. The Princess thinks I am cooking it but I am really giving it a bubble bath and a good meal. Then I send it back out to the grounds and give the Princess a whole different sandwich. I have already saved a few species today!"

And "the dress! Well, what better to dress our Princess in than tinfoil jewels and a dress of trash. I think she'll be quite surprised!"

The very next day, the Prince called the Princess to the Royal Hall of Mirrors. **"Princess, your wedding hat is ready! Would you please come try it on?"** He sent the Jester to go find her but they were back in only two seconds. The Princess was not far away because she had been in the Hall of Mirrors only just before, admiring herself.

"Here it is! Ta, da!" said the Prince. "The kingdom's finest artisans worked on it all day and night."

"I'm speechless," she gasped.

"It's, it's, it's wonderful!" she exclaimed, seeing her reflection in the mirror. "I'm so beautiful! What is this amazing animal anyway? I really don't recognize it! It must be the rarest of rare."

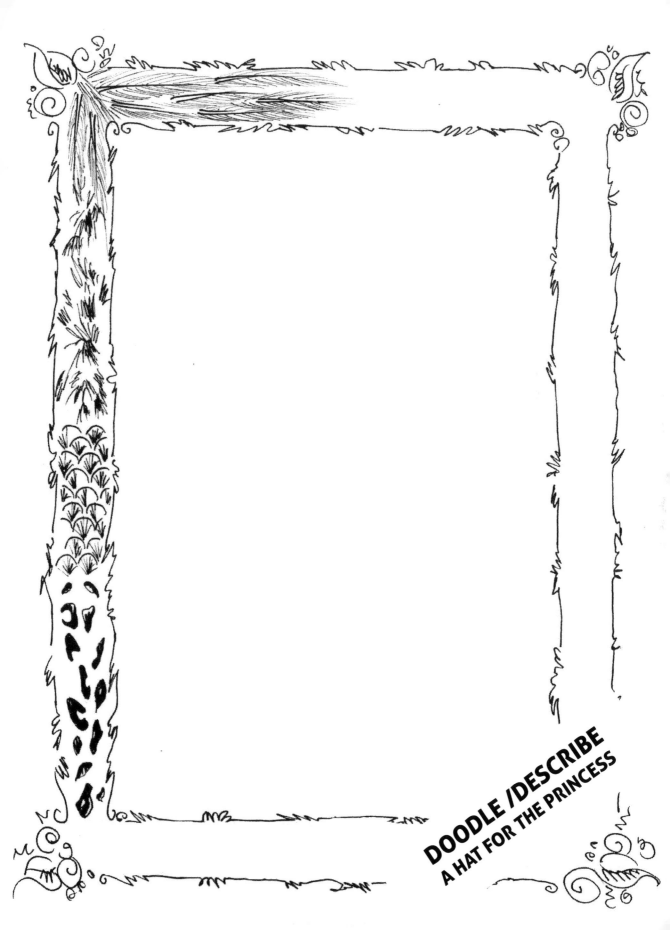

DOODLE /DESCRIBE
A HAT FOR THE PRINCESS

"This is our finest of materials. It's recycling! It's all the rage in Snizz! But it's not made from rare animals. It takes the creativity of many, many people to make it possible. That is why it is so precious."

"Well, I love it! Anything this precious is perfect for a Princess! I want my whole dress made like this! Thank you. Thank you very much!"

"Really?" said the Prince. "Well then, we'll do our best for you. Your dress design will match this hat. Our finest artisans are working on it." The Prince thought to himself, "Hey, maybe she might be coming around? Perhaps I should tell her about swapping her sandwiches too?"

Just then the Princess's stomach growled loudly! "I'm suddenly so hungry!" she said.

"Let's call in the Chef to make everyone a sandwich! Chef, CHEF!"

"Uh, Princess, let me go and help you find him," said the Prince. "Good, he thought, this might be the perfect time to tell her."

Quick as a wink, the Prince was back, although a little out of breath and tongue tied!

"Princess, I'm the Prince, I mean the Designer, I mean…"

"Chef!" reminded the Jester.

"Oh, yes — that 's right! Well now, Princess, I heard you were hungry? I'll make you something right away," said the Prince, "but I have something to tell you."

DOODLE /DESCRIBE
THE CREATURE IN THE BUBBLEBATH

"It can wait, Chef," she said. "Right now, I just want to eat...and I love your cooking!"

"What a relief, Your Highness! I shall always be your cook," said the Prince, feeling even better about telling her the truth.

"OK, then let's go pick out one of those creatures together right now," she said, remembering her plan. "Get your net ready!"

"Sure," said the Prince. "And he winked to the Jester to ready the animal's bubble bath!"

As the Prince and Princess walked out into the garden, the King passed them by. "Has anyone seen the Prince?"

"No," said the Prince.

"Hmmm," said the King. "That guy looks so familiar!"

Later that day, the Jester brought the Prince to the Princess's room, disguised as the Royal Architect.

"PRINCESS, PRINCESS! I HAVE DESIGNED AND MADE THE PERFECT HOME FOR YOU!"

"You work so fast! Where is it? Mountaintop?" she asked as she looked out her window hoping to find it.

"YES!" he said, but she looked and looked and did not see a thing.

So she asked again, thinking maybe he did not hear her.

"Beach?" she asked.

"Yes," said the Prince.

She looked and looked and still didn't see anything. "Valley?" she said with a look of confusion.

"Yes!"

"But I don't see anything!" she sighed.

The Prince held out a bag of many colors. "Here ya go!" he said.

"OK, now let's go see them!"

"You have it!" said the Prince. "Your new home!"

"This is a bag!" said the Princess. "Princesses do not live in bags! Especially not this one!"

"Your home is not the bag," said the Prince. "It's in the bag! Inside is the best home for you because you can see the stars from your bed. You can sleep in the mountains, valleys, beaches, and anywhere else you heart desires!"

As the Princess opened the bag, pieces and parts fell out all over the place.

"It's a t–t–t–t–tent!" But the Princess was brave and she tried to compromise. "OK, well, if you decorate it with sparkles and fancy designs, and you help me set it up, I guess I could try it."

"I'd love to!" said the Prince. And off they went.

The next morning, the Princess wandered back to the castle. It was breakfast time.

The Prince was ready to greet her, dressed as the Chef.

"You know, Princess, I just found another one of those snarklecats. Do you want it now or shall I save it for the wedding feast?"

The Princess sat quietly looking out the castle window as if she did not hear him.

"I'm not hungry," she said.

THE PRINCE LOOKED AT HER AND NOTICED HOW SAD SHE LOOKED.

"What's wrong?"

"Well, I don't know if I'll really be getting married and staying in this kingdom," she said.

"Why?" asked the Prince.

"Because the Prince is missing!" She said bursting into tears. "No one knows where he is and I have begun to really like it here. I mean, I was hoping they'd have some more shoe stores and stuff, but it turns out that this place is really quite pretty, and then last night, I slept in that tent. I thought it would be awful. But the birds were singing and the moonlight was shining and the air was so clear, I really didn't want to go home anymore either. Even if we do have a great big super deluxe mall with everything a Princess could ever buy."

The Prince was bursting with joy. He could not hold in his secrets any longer!

"Well, I have a surprise for you!" he said.

Guessing it was a sandwich, the Princess replied, "No thanks. I really do not feel hungry right now."

"No, not that kind of surprise," said the Prince, and he pulled out a fluffy pillow from under his Chef's coat.

"You're skinny?" said the Princess. "That's the surprise?"

"That's not all," said the Prince and he ripped off his skinny mustache!

"You're hairless?" asked the Princess.

The Prince smiled and laughed, "No! I am really the Crown Prince of Snizz!"

The Princess said, "Forgive me, your... Majesty!" as she curtsied low before the Prince.

"It's OK, Princess," he said with a huge smile on his face. "You have been a good sport and I am happy to see you."

"Why did you do this?" she asked.

"I wanted to get to know you," said the Prince, "and to see whether you would be happy living here. We do things differently in Snizz. And I really couldn't love someone who ate our royal pets and destroyed our environment!"

The Princess turned a shade of white, "Oh my gosh — the royal pets — I ate them!!!"

"No, no, you never ate them! I was switching your meals each and every time," he replied. All the animals are safe and sound and happy in the new and wonderful ZOOPOSSIBLE that's been built in honor of our wedding this very afternoon!"

"The wedding!" She smiled and sparkled all over. "Oh — no my gown!"

"It will be ready today! Just in time for our wedding. Shall we go bake the cake?"

"Together!" exclaimed the Princess, and she put the skinny mustache under her nose and followed the Prince to the Royal Kitchen.

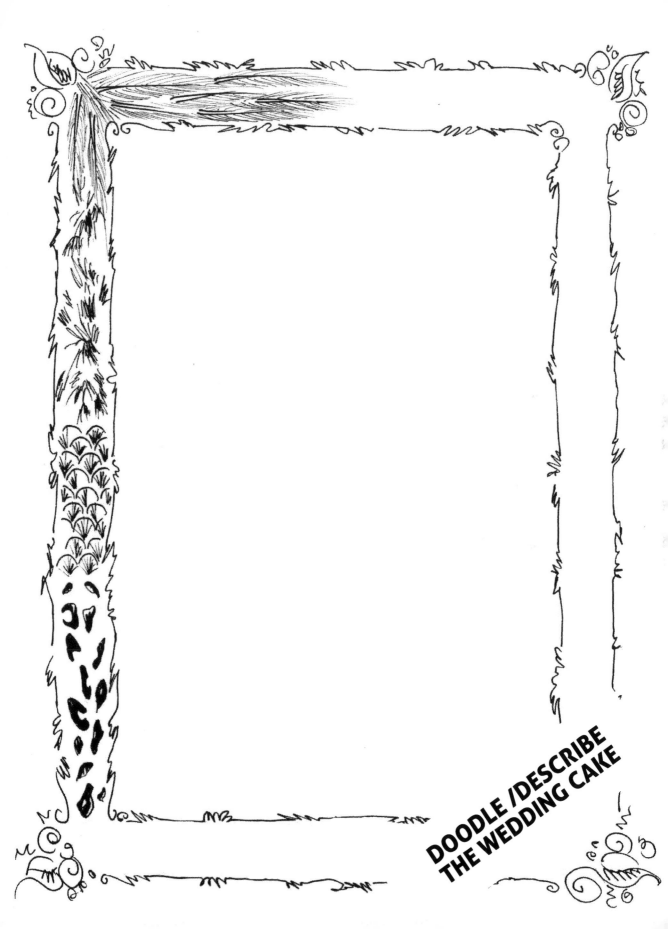

DOODLE /DESCRIBE
THE WEDDING CAKE

That afternoon, the whole kingdom gathered in the castle garden. The King came out of the castle and stood in front of the new gates of ZOOPOSSIBLE.

"Citizens and animals of Snizz," he said. "For every grand announcement in the kingdom, our royal trumpets sing DO, DA, DOO! But I am afraid to say that today we will have no trumpets, and we will have no wedding because, alas, we have no Prince. Booo, hoo," he cried.

As the first tear rolled down upon the King's cheek, the Jester flipped into the air and leapt in front of the King. "Yes, we do, your highness! Trumpets," he shouted, "Announce the Prince!"

"DO, DA, DOO!" went the royal trumpets, and just like magic, the Prince made his royal entrance waving and smiling to the King and all the animals and citizens of Snizz. "Hello, Dad," he said. "I am sorry I have been away." He took off a sparkly safari hat and bowed in front of the King.

"Son, I've been looking for you everywhere! I am so happy to see you. You have arrived just in time, for it's your wedding day!"

"Trumpets," said the King, "announce the Bride!"

"DO, DA, DOO," went the trumpets. The Princess came out to the garden smiling from ear to ear in a sparkly dress made of recycled trash.

"Let's do this thing!" said the Princess.

"Hooray!" shouted the crowd.

"Let's begin," said the King. "Trumpets! Announce the royal wedding rituals!"

"DO, DA, DOO," went the trumpets.

The Bride took a bite of the cake that she and the Prince had made together, and she professed her love for Snizz and the Prince. "I will care for all of Snizz... and I will always eat your cooking!" she said. The Prince took a bite of cake and confessed his love in return. "I will always care for you because you are one of a kind."

"Trumpets!" proclaimed the King, "Announce the Royal Kiss!"

"Ewwww!" said the Jester!

"Oh, really. It's not that bad," said the Prince.

"It's better than kissing a frog like those other fairy tales!" said the Princess.

And with that, the Jester popped up smiling between the two, receiving the Royal Kiss on each cheek.

"Presenting the new Royal Couple!" announced the King.

"Triple!" Jester joked. "Hey, doesn't this wedding have any dancing?"

"Oh, my favorite part!" said the King. "It's time to go wild in ZOOPOSSIBLE!" And with that, all the animals and people followed the King, putting on the razzamatazz as they danced into the sunset.

Made in the USA
Charleston, SC
08 December 2013